Zug the Bug

Colin and Jacqui Hawkins

DK

DORLING KINDERSLEY
London • New York • Stuttgart

Have you heard of Zug the bug?

b

He went fishing with a dog called Pug.

When their rod gave a tug . .

. . . out of the water popped a big fat slug!

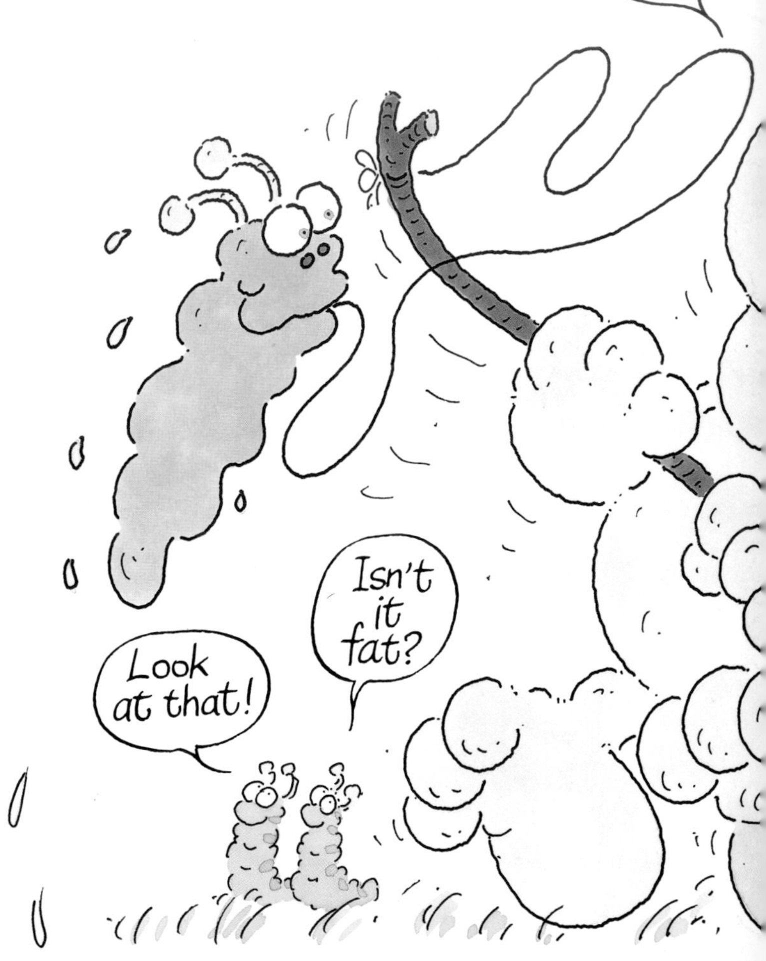

"We've caught a slug!" said Zug. So Pug and Zug did hop and hug.

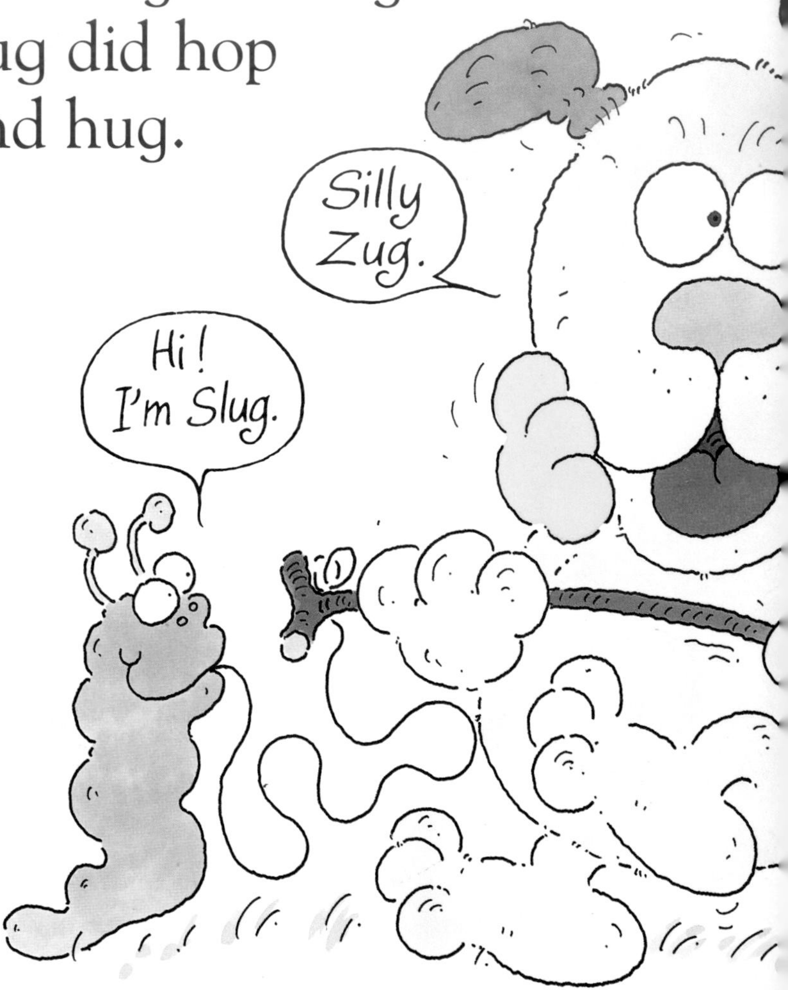

"Let's take Slug home," said Zug, and they put him in an old milk jug.

Slug, inside the jug, was very hard for them to lug.

1

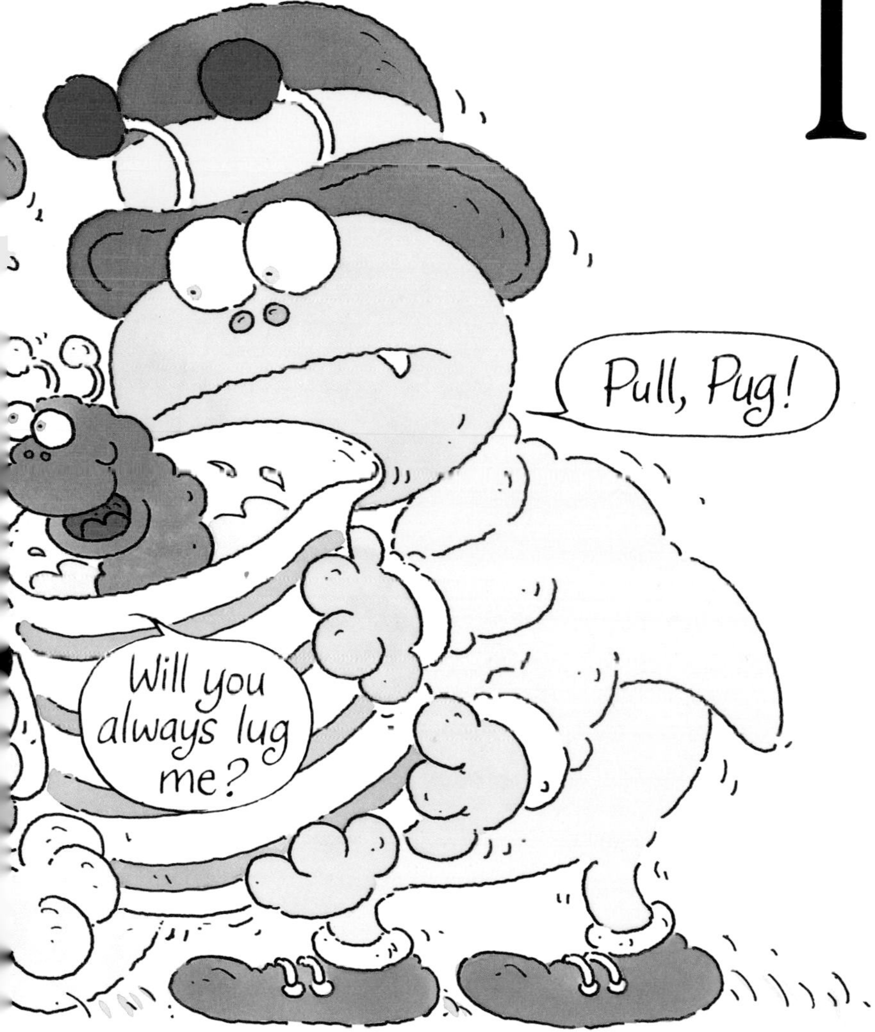

Home at last with Slug,
they all had milk
from a big tin mug.

Then, warm and snug, Zug, Pug, and Slug went to sleep on a bright red rug.

A DORLING KINDERSLEY BOOK

Published in the United Kingdom in 1995
by Dorling Kindersley Limited,
9 Henrietta Street, London WC2E 8PS

Published in the United States in 1995
by Dorling Kindersley Publishing, Inc.,
95 Madison Avenue, New York, New York 10016

2 4 6 8 10 9 7 5 3

Text and illustrations copyright © 1988 Colin and Jacqui Hawkins

ISBN 0-7513-5349-3 (UK)
ISBN 0-7894-0155-X (US)

Reproduction by DOT Gradations
Printed in Italy by L.E.G.O.